EMMA GIGGLED

Written and illustrated by LOU ALPERT

Whispering Coyote Press Inc./New York

Published by Whispering Coyote Press Inc.
P.O. Box 2159, Halesite, New York 11743-2159
Text copyright © 1991 by Lou Alpert
Illustrations copyright © 1991 by Lou Alpert
All rights reserved including the right of
reproduction in whole or in part or in any form.
Printed in the United States of America
ISBN 1-879085-06-2

To my children,
who make me GIGGLE!

Ian

Angie

Regan

Dan

Emma

Mickey

Max

Emma woke up, stretched, and stumbled into the hallway.

It was Tuesday morning, just like any other morning.

Suddenly, she heard a CRASH! and a YELL!

Emma looked downstairs just in time to see her dad leap for their dog Baxter.

Now Emma knew this was not funny. Baxter is a BIG dog! He could make a BIG mess!

Emma thought about her dad running after
Baxter. Then something started to happen. It began
deep in her stomach and rose like lava in a volcano.
Her body shook, her stomach jiggled — all at once
Emma GIGGLED!

Emma stood at the top of the stairs trying to control the eruptions in her belly. Bounding down from the attic came her brother Ian. "Hi Booper, how are you this morning?" he said.

Emma looked at Ian and her lips began to wiggle. Emma couldn't speak a word — Emma could only GIGGLE!

Laying on the floor, Emma grabbed her middle.
She thought that if she squeezed just right, she could
stop those crazy giggles.

As Emma closed her eyes and took a deep breath,
she heard a familiar voice. "Mom, have you seen my
hairbrush?" It was her sister Angie.

Then it started again, from way down in her toes.
She tried to stop, she swallowed hard, but still that
feeling rose — and Emma GIGGLED!

As she tried to get control of herself, Emma
heard her mom calling from the kitchen,
"EVERYONE COME TO BREAKFAST!"

Emma bounced down the stairs. When she reached the bottom, there stood her brother Mickey in their dad's shoes with a towel on his head. "Shoes!" he said.

Emma looked at Mickey with his shoes and with his curls. As if she'd never stopped at all, her head began to whirl — and Emma GIGGLED!

Mickey watched as Emma rolled back and forth
on the floor.

Then before you could count "1-2-3" Mickey started to chuckle, both ears began to wiggle. It happened all at once — and little Mickey GIGGLED!

Emma heard her mom yelling, "Dan, please go get Emma and Mickey for breakfast or we'll all be late for school." When Dan found them, they couldn't even talk. Emma would giggle faster and Mickey would giggle louder.

As Dan sat down to watch them, wondering what to say, he felt a tingling in his toes that wouldn't go away — and Dan GIGGLED!

By now Mom was losing her patience and breakfast was getting cold. "Angie, would you please find everyone and get them to the table?" she said.

Angie could hear giggling before she reached the stairs. In a loud voice she said, "Get to breakfast NOW!"

Mickey, Emma, and Dan marched to the table.

They had no sooner started to eat when Mickey
stood up in his high chair and began to shake his
head. Emma looked at Dan and their eyes began to
glimmer, their noses started twitching, their lips
began to shimmer — and Emma and Dan GIGGLED.

Mom pleaded across the kitchen, "Would you please stop that giggling and eat your breakfast? It's almost eight o'clock, and we'll never get to school on time."

Now even Ian and Angie finally lost their cool.
Consumed by the giggles — they forgot about school!

Mom stood there looking over this giggling heap of kids. She tried to look stern, but what could she do? She felt the giggles coming on too!

Mom started to speak, her mouth made a curl,
her eyebrows wiggled, she did a little twirl — and
Mom GIGGLED!

And that's where Dad found them, collapsed in a
pile. He didn't quite giggle — but he sure did smile!